SPECIAL THANKS TO
ANNE MARIE RYAN

ORCHARD BOOKS
Carmelite House
50 Victoria Embankment
London EC4Y 0DZ

First published by Orchard Books in 2018

A CIP catalogue record for this book is available
from the British Library.

ISBN 978 1 40835 319 6

1 3 5 7 9 10 8 6 4 2

Printed in China

Orchard Books
An imprint of Hachette Children's Group
Part of The Watts Publishing Group Limited
An Hachette UK Company
www.hachette.co.uk

BUBBLES'S
UNICORN FRIEND

ORCHARD

BLOSSOM

Blossom is the leader of the Powerpuff Girls. She loves being organised. Her favourite colour is pink. Blossom can fly and has ice breath.

BUBBLES

Bubbles is the kindest Powerpuff Girl. She loves animals, computers and make-up. Her favourite colour is blue. Bubbles can fly and talk to animals.

BUTTERCUP

Buttercup is the fiercest Powerpuff Girl. She likes rockets and tanks. Her favourite colour is green. Buttercup can fly and is very strong.

DONNY

Donny is a unicorn. He likes glitter and sparkles. He can do magic.

CONTENTS

PART ONE: A UNICORN VISITOR

PART TWO: CHELSEA

PART THREE: MOJO JOJO'S PLAN

PART ONE
A Unicorn Visitor

CHAPTER ONE

He's Coming!

"Yay!" said Bubbles. "He's coming today!" She flew around the living room excitedly. She had to get everything ready.

First she blew up balloons. Next she hung up a banner.

Then she put out a tray of tasty snacks and drinks.

"Who is coming today?" her sister Buttercup asked.

"Donny!" said Bubbles.

"How could you forget?" said her other sister, Blossom.

Bubbles had been talking about it for days. Donny the Unicorn was Bubbles's best friend. He was coming to stay with the Powerpuff Girls for a whole week! He was even going to go to school with them. Bubbles couldn't wait for him to arrive. She wanted everything to be perfect. She had planned lots of fun things to do with Donny.

DING DONG!

"He is here!" squealed Bubbles happily.

She flew to the door and opened it. A white unicorn with a yellow mane was standing outside. He was holding two suitcases and a sleeping bag.

"Donny!" cried Bubbles. She gave her unicorn friend a hug.

Donny was really excited to see his best friend.

"We're going to have a great time," Bubbles said. She told her friend about all the cool things they would do together.

"We'll draw pictures together," said Bubbles.

"Awesome!" said Donny.

"We'll eat ice cream together," said Bubbles.

"Yum!" said Donny.

"And we'll sing songs together," said Bubbles.

"Yippee!" cried out Donny.

"It's going to be amazing!"

Donny gave Bubbles another hug. Then he gave Bubbles a present. It was a very special unicorn spoon with a bow and a unicorn tail.

Bubbles loved it!

"This is going to be the best week ever!" Bubbles said happily.

CHAPTER TWO

Donny Goes to School

The next day, Donny went to school with the Powerpuff Girls.

"Hi, everyone," said Bubbles proudly. "This is my best friend, Donny."

All the children thought it was cool to meet a unicorn!

BRIIIINNGG! The school bell rang. Donny and Bubbles were in different classes.

"I'll meet you here after school, Donny," said Bubbles.

As she flew to her classroom, Bubbles felt a bit worried.

"I hope Donny will be OK," she said.

After school, Bubbles, Blossom and Buttercup waited for Donny.

"Here he comes!" said Blossom.

The unicorn's tail swished from side to side as he trotted down the hall.

"How was your day?" asked Bubbles.

"It was great!" said Donny cheerfully. "Everyone was really nice to me."

Bubbles was glad that Donny had enjoyed school. She showed him her pens. "Let's go home and do some drawing," she suggested.

"Sorry, Bubbles," said Donny. "I did some drawing earlier. My new friend Chelsea has a big pack of glitter pens." He held up a sparkly picture he had coloured.

"Who is Chelsea?" asked Bubbles.

"She is in my class," said Donny. "She is really funny."

"Well, maybe we could go roller skating," said Bubbles.

"I went roller skating with Chelsea at school," said Donny. "It was lots of fun!"

Bubbles felt left out. "You did all that without me?" she said sadly.

RING! RING!

Donny answered his phone.

"Hi, Chelsea!" he said. "I will meet you at Penguin Pete's Ice Cream Shop. See you soon!"

Donny hung up the phone and waved goodbye to the Powerpuff Girls. "I have got to go! I am meeting Chelsea for ice cream."

As Donny trotted off, Bubbles's eyes filled with tears.

She had been left out of the fun AGAIN!

CHAPTER THREE

Bubbles Gets Jealous

Back at home, Bubbles felt
very upset. She took out her
new pens and drew a sad face.
Then she scribbled all over her
picture. Drawing was no fun
without Donny!

Donny is having fun without me, thought Bubbles.

They were supposed to draw pictures and go roller skating together. But instead of spending time with Bubbles, Donny was eating ice cream with Chelsea!

Thinking about Donny and his new friend having fun made Bubbles feel angry. She snapped one of her new pens in half. But that didn't make her feel any better.

"It is not fair!" she wailed.

Bubbles's sisters tried to comfort her.

"What's wrong, Bubbles?" asked Blossom.

"Donny is doing all the fun things I had planned," said Bubbles. "But he's doing them with Chelsea, instead of me!"

"Don't be jealous," said Blossom. "Donny is allowed to make new friends."

"You shouldn't worry about Chelsea," said Buttercup. "Donny is still your best friend. You two have lots in common."

It was true. Donny and Bubbles liked all of the same things. They both loved stickers and rainbows and glitter. They even liked the same foods!

"You might like Chelsea too," said Buttercup.

Suddenly, Bubbles felt a lot better. Her sisters were right.

"Why don't we go and meet her?" Blossom suggested.

"That's a good idea," Bubbles said. She smiled at her sister. Blossom always came up with great plans!

Bubbles couldn't wait to meet Chelsea. Maybe they could all be friends.

PART TWO
CHELSEA

CHAPTER FOUR

Penguin Pete's Ice Cream Shop

WHOOSH! The Powerpuff Girls flew to Penguin Pete's Ice Cream Shop. They found Donny sitting at a table.

"Hi, Bubbles," said Donny in surprise. "What are you guys doing here?"

"We wanted to meet Chelsea," said Bubbles. "She sounds really nice."

The Powerpuff Girls sat down at Donny's table.

"I'm starving," said Buttercup. "I'm going to get a big banana split with sprinkles and nuts." Buttercup was always hungry!

"Just a scoop of strawberry for me," said Blossom. She liked everything pink.

"Chelsea and I are going to share a chocolate sundae," Donny told them.

Bubbles felt jealous again. She wanted to be the one sharing an ice cream with Donny!

A cute girl with blue hair came over. She was holding a big bowl full of ice cream.

She sat down next to Donny.

"This is Chelsea," Donny told the Powerpuff Girls.

"Hi, everyone!" said Chelsea. She smiled sweetly. "Your friends are cool, Donny!"

Donny hugged his new friend. "Isn't Chelsea adorable?"

"Hey, guys," said Chelsea. "Want to hear a song I wrote with Donny?"

"*It's magic, we are friends, best friends!*" they sang.

Now Bubbles felt REALLY, REALLY, REALLY jealous!

"We'd better eat our ice cream before it melts," said Chelsea. She got out a spoon and took a bite.

Bubbles gasped. Donny had given Chelsea a special unicorn spoon, too!

Now Bubbles wasn't just jealous. She was ANGRY!

CHAPTER FIVE

Bubbles and Donny Have a Fight

TICK TOCK! TICK TOCK!

It was very late. Bubbles sat alone in the dark. She was waiting for Donny to come home. She got more and more angry as she waited.

Bubbles imagined all the fun Donny was having with Chelsea.

At last the front door opened and Donny came in.

"Where have you been?" Bubbles asked.

"Chelsea and I went to see *Space Towtruck on Ice*," Donny said. "It was amazing!"

That made Bubbles really cross. *Space Towtruck* was her favourite television show! And she loved ice skating! She flew over to Donny.

"I can't believe you went without me!" yelled Bubbles.

Donny was confused. "Why are you angry?" he asked.

"Because you keep leaving me out," said Bubbles.

"Chelsea has invited us both to a sleepover," said Donny.

"But if you keep acting jealous I will go on my own."

"Fine! Go to Chelsea's!" shouted Bubbles. "I don't care!"

But she did care. She thought that Donny liked Chelsea more than her. That hurt her feelings.

"You are not my best friend any more!" Bubbles told Donny.

She took out the special unicorn spoon Donny had given her. Using her super strength, Bubbles bent the spoon. Then she threw it on the floor.

Donny gasped. "You are not my best friend," he yelled. "You are the worst friend ever!"

SLAM! Donny left, banging the door shut behind him.

CHAPTER SIX

Bubbles Blubs

Tears ran down Bubbles's cheeks. She missed Donny so much! She had never argued with him before. Bubbles thought she had lost her best friend for ever.

Bubbles sobbed and sobbed and sobbed. She cried until her eyes were red and sore.

Her sisters were worried about her. They tried to cheer her up.

"You can just tell Donny that you are sorry," said Blossom.

"Waaaaaaaa!" sobbed Bubbles.

She had said lots of mean things to Donny. She had even bent the special unicorn spoon he had given her. Would Donny ever forgive her?

"Don't worry," Buttercup said. "Donny still loves you. A real friend will forgive you if you say sorry."

Bubbles wasn't so sure. "But Chelsea is amazing," she wailed. "She is so cute."

"You are cute," said Blossom.

"Chelsea can sing really well," sobbed Bubbles.

"You have a great voice, too," said Buttercup.

"Chelsea lives in a volcano," cried Bubbles.

"Wait a minute," said Blossom. "The only volcano nearby belongs to—"

"Mojo Jojo!" gasped Buttercup.

Mojo Jojo was always coming up with evil plans.

He wanted to take over Townsville, where the Powerpuff Girls lived.

"Oh no!" cried Bubbles. "Chelsea must work for Mojo Jojo! Donny is in danger. We have to save him!"

PART THREE
Mojo Jojo's Plan

CHAPTER SEVEN

The Cutest Robot Ever

The Powerpuff Girls flew into the air. They had to rescue Donny!

SMASH! CRASH! BASH! Blossom, Buttercup and Bubbles crashed into the volcano.

"Oh no!" said Bubbles. "Poor Donny!"

The unicorn was hanging in the air. His horn was connected to a machine. Unicorn magic flowed from his horn into the machine.

"Help me, Bubbles!" cried Donny.

Mojo Jojo rubbed his hands together gleefully. "My evil plan is working perfectly!" he said. "Soon I will be able to destroy Townsville!"

"Let my best friend go!" Bubbles shouted at Mojo Jojo.

But Mojo laughed. "Chelsea, come here!" the bad monkey called out.

The cute blue-haired girl came into the room.

"Hi, friends!" she said cheerfully.

Then Chelsea twirled around and around in the air. As she spun, Chelsea's body changed into metal.

The Powerpuff Girls gasped in shock. Chelsea was a robot!

"Chelsea tricked that silly unicorn into coming here for a sleepover," Mojo Jojo said.

"Why are you doing this?" asked Blossom.

"I need unicorn magic to power my Death Ray," said Mojo Jojo. "Once I have taken all of his magic, I will rule Townsville!"

The bad monkey let out an evil laugh. "*MWAH HA HA!*"

CHAPTER EIGHT

A Big Battle

The Powerpuff Girls had to stop Mojo Jojo. They could not let him take Donny's magic. But first, they needed a plan.

"Bubbles, you help Donny," shouted Blossom. "Buttercup and I will deal with Chelsea!"

Buttercup narrowed her green eyes and flew at Chelsea with all of her super speed.

"Do you want to do some drawing?" Chelsea asked. "I have glitter!"

Lots of glittery sparkles flew out of the robot's hands.

She hit Buttercup with a blast
of glitter.

BLAM! Buttercup slammed
into the volcano's wall.

"Hold on, Buttercup," shouted
Blossom. "I am coming!"

Blossom flew at the cute
robot using every bit of her
super strength.

"It's time to do colouring!"
said Chelsea, laughing.

The robot's fingers turned
into colourful pens. Then she
punched Blossom!

POW! Blossom hit the wall.

At the same time, Bubbles was busy rescuing Donny. She flew up and released him, then gently put him down on the ground. Donny was free!

"Are you OK?" Bubbles asked Donny.

"I'm fine," said Donny.

Bubbles hugged her best friend. She was so relieved that Donny was safe.

But he wasn't safe for long …

"Crush that Powerpuff Girl!" Mojo Jojo ordered Chelsea the robot. "And her silly unicorn friend, too!"

CHAPTER NINE

Best Friends Again

Bubbles climbed on to Donny's back. She held on to his mane.

"Come on, Donny," said Bubbles. "We can fight Chelsea and Mojo Jojo together!"

"Donny is not your best friend," Chelsea the robot said.

"Oh yes, he is," said Bubbles. She held up her bent unicorn spoon proudly. "I have the spoon to prove it!"

"That silly spoon won't save you!" said Chelsea.

FLASH!

Pink light shot from the robot's eyes. The laser beams sped straight towards Donny and Bubbles!

ZAP! The light hit Bubbles's spoon. It blasted back towards Chelsea.

KABOOM! The robot broke. They had defeated her!

Bubbles went over to help her sisters.

SMASH! Donny and Bubbles crashed into the controls for Mojo Jojo's death ray.

ZAP! The ray hit Mojo Jojo.

It burned the bad monkey on his bottom. Mojo Jojo ran away.

The Powerpuff Girls and Donny had saved the day!

Donny and Bubbles had a big hug.

"I'm sorry I got jealous," said Bubbles. "It's OK to have lots of friends."

"I'm sorry too," said Donny. "I made you feel left out."

"I know how to celebrate beating Chelsea," Blossom said. "Let's go out for ice cream!"

The rest of the week was really fun, but soon it was time for Donny to go home. Bubbles gave Donny a scrapbook. It had pictures of all the fun things they had done together.

Donny loved it!

"Goodbye!" said Blossom and Buttercup.

"I'll miss you, Donny," said Bubbles.

"I'll miss you too," said Donny. "This has been the best week ever!"

Bubbles hugged Donny goodbye. She knew they would always be friends.

THE END

Well done!

You have finished this book.
You are super fierce, just like
the Powerpuff Girls!